S0-EKB-178

Celebrity
Biographies

Johnny Depp

MOVIE MEGASTAR

JILL MENKES KUSHNER

Enslow Publishers, Inc.
40 Industrial Road
Box 398
Berkeley Heights, NJ 07922
USA
http://www.enslow.com

Library of Congress Cataloging-in-Publication Data
Kushner, Jill Menkes.
  Johnny Depp : movie megastar / by Jill Menkes Kushner.
    p. cm.
  Includes bibliographical references and index.
  Summary: "Read about Johnny Depp's life—from his early tv to the star of hit movies"—Provided by publisher.
  ISBN-13: 978-0-7660-3567-6
  ISBN-10: 0-7660-3567-0
  1. Depp, Johnny—Juvenile literature. 2. Motion picture actors and actresses—United States—Biography—Juvenile
literature. I. Title.
  PN2287.D39K87 2009
  791.4302'8'092—dc22
  [B]
                              2008051093

Paperback ISBN-13: 978-0-7660-3631-4
Paperback ISBN-10: 0-7660-3631-6

Printed in the United States of America

10 9 8 7 6 5 4 3 2 1

To our readers: We have done our best to make sure all Internet Addresses in this book were active and appropriate when we went to press. However, the author and the publisher have no control over and assume no liability for the material available on those Internet sites or on other Web sites they may link to. Any comments or suggestions can be sent by e-mail to comments@enslow.com or to the address on the back cover.

♻ Enslow Publishers, Inc., is committed to printing our books on recycled paper. The paper in every book contains 10% to 30% post-consumer waste (PCW). The cover board on the outside of each book contains 100% PCW. Our goal is to do our part to help young people and the environment too!

Photographs: Matt Sayles/AP Images, 1; Luis Martinez/AP Images, 4; Damian Dovarganes/AP Images, 7; Jim Smeal/WireImage/Getty Images, 8; Michael Ochs Archives/Stringer/Getty Images, 11; Barry King/WireImage/Getty Images, 13, 14; Fotos International/Getty Images, 17; Michel Euler/AP Images, 19; Zade Rosenthal/Twentieth Century Fox/Photofest, 21; Rhonda Birndorf/AP Images, 22; MGM/Photofest, 24; Ron Galella, Ltd./Getty Images, 25; Francois Mori/AP Images, 27; Remy de la Mauviniere/AP Images, 28, 29; Reed Saxon/AP Images, 31; Chris Pizzello/AP Images, 34; Buena Vista Pictures/Photofest, 37; Kevork Djansezian/AP Images, 43

Cover photo: Johnny Depp arrives at the premiere of *Sweeney Todd: The Demon Barber of Fleet Street* in December 2007. Matt Sayles/AP Images.

Contents

Childhood: Fantasy and Reality

Johnny Depp is certainly not an average movie star. He's been called different, offbeat, and even weird. That might be part of the reason he has stayed popular for so many years. He brings a fresh take to every new role and surprises audiences again and again.

Sometimes, he even surprises his producers and directors. When Depp showed up to film *Pirates of the Caribbean*, the film's producers rolled their eyes. He had covered all of his teeth in gold! Disney might have been picturing a more traditional pirate for the movie, which came out in 2003. But Depp had his own ideas on how to play the role of Jack Sparrow. Depp's pirate was wacky, staggering, and unpredictable.

In 2004, Depp switched gears. He played children's author James M. Barrie in the movie *Finding Neverland*. Barrie

◀ *Johnny Depp is pictured at the world premiere of* Charlie and the Chocolate Factory *in 2005.*

ALL ABOUT JOHNNY

Full name: John Christopher Depp II

Birthday: June 9, 1963

Height: 5 feet 9 inches

Hair: Dark brown

Eyes: Brown

Childhood ambition: To be a musician

Interests: Reading, making music, and spending time with his two children, Lily-Rose and Jack

wrote the famous play *Peter Pan. Finding Neverland* tells the story of Barrie as he meets a young widow and her four children. As Barrie grows closer to the family, he is inspired to write *Peter Pan.*

Depp's next role also put him around children, but in a completely different way. He played Willy Wonka in *Charlie and the Chocolate Factory* in 2005. Wonka is the rich, strange owner of a secretive chocolate factory. When five children win a tour, Wonka rewards or punishes their behavior in unusual ways.

While these are three very different movies, fans might have noticed a common theme. Since Depp became a father himself, he has made a string of movies involving adventure, fantasy, and childish flights of imagination. Both the young and the young at heart enjoy these movies.

THE DEPP FAMILY

Johnny Depp's own childhood was far from lighthearted, though. From a young age, Johnny struggled with feeling insecure. He was born in Owensboro, Kentucky, on June 9, 1963. His parents named him John Christopher Depp II. Everyone called him Johnny from an early

▲ *Johnny Depp poses for a photo in 2003.*

age. Johnny had three older siblings: a sister Christi, and two half-siblings, Danny and Debbie. Depp's family background is part Native American, part Irish, and part German.

7

▲ *Johnny Depp attends a premiere with his mother, Betty Sue Palmer.*

His hometown of Owensboro is located 180 miles southeast of St. Louis, Missouri, and 120 miles north of Nashville, Tennessee. The Depp family had a long history in the area. Johnny's grandfather was a civil engineer there after World War II. He started the firm Johnson, Depp & Quisenberry with two other partners.

Johnny's family lived in a modest home. His father, John, worked with his father as a civil engineer. Johnny's mother, Betty Sue, worked as a waitress.

Johnny was very close to his mother. He also maintained a close relationship with his maternal grandfather, a Cherokee, until he died in 1970. Johnny called his grandfather PawPaw. PawPaw taught him to fish and farm tobacco. More than any other adult, his grandfather was a role model for Johnny, guiding him. Depp has said he feels a close connection to the man who spent so much time with him and clearly loved him deeply.

MOVING AROUND

In 1970, the Depp family moved to Miramar, Florida. Miramar was a small city near Miami, very different from the country landscape of Kentucky. There, Johnny started a lifelong friendship with Sal Jenco, who would also become an actor. When the Depps first came to Miramar, the family lived in a hotel while Johnny's father sought work.

"We moved like gypsies," Depp has said. He remembers his family living in "thirty or forty houses," plus a motel and a farm. As a result of all the moves, the young Johnny was always changing schools. Sometimes, he would not even introduce himself to other kids, because he figured he would be moving again soon. "My mom just liked to move for some reason," he said. "It was hard. . . . We never stayed in one neighborhood for long. At the drop of a hat, we'd go."

BECOMING A PIRATE

Johnny Depp does a lot of research before playing a role. He prepared for the role of Jack Sparrow in the movie *Pirates of the Caribbean* by reading all about pirates. "Research is at least half the fun," Depp told a reporter during an interview with *Rolling Stone* in 2006. "It's like studying for a history exam. The nutrition onboard those ships, that was a real eye-opener. They'd eat by candlelight, below deck, and be so sickened by the food that they'd blow out the candles so they didn't have to see the maggots."

He had difficulty making new friends and spent time watching old movies. He became a fan of horror movies at an early age.

Johnny's home life was noisy and chaotic. His parents fought a lot. In addition, his brother Danny played the music of Bob Dylan and Van Morrison on the stereo—at full blast. When he was young, Johnny assumed that all families were like his—always on the move, with parents who argued.

His family did not eat together. Usually, everyone would just grab a sandwich on the go. Sometimes Johnny would visit his friend Sal Jenco, whose house was much calmer. When he was there, Johnny felt as though he was on a different planet. He longed for a sense of home and a feeling of safety. In his

▲ *Growing up, Johnny Depp listened to the music of Bob Dylan.*

own home, he said later, "I felt loved, but I also felt hated."

COMFORT IN MUSIC

When Johnny was twelve years old, his mother bought him his first guitar. It was electric. He loved music and practiced constantly, teaching himself completely on his own. His first musical inspiration had been his uncle, who was a preacher. Johnny loved the way gospel music could inspire people.

As he got better at playing guitar, his musical tastes began to expand. He liked the songs of rockers Peter Frampton, Tom Waits, and Aerosmith. The wild behavior of the band Kiss appealed to him. He listened to the Clash, David Bowie, and Iggy Pop. Depp imitated the style of Eddie Van Halen. He would listen to records and recreate the sounds he wanted. Johnny even liked the classical music of Mozart and Brahms. At that age, he thought music was his future.

SPLITTING UP

Johnny's parents divorced when he was fifteen years old. He remembers being relieved when they split up. It was something he had been expecting to happen for years.

Depp was actually surprised that they were able to stay together for as long as they did. His parents' breakup had a lasting influence on him. From that point in his life, he would always be looking for the security of a stable family.

After his parents' divorce, Depp's mother became ill. Depp took care of her until her health improved. He saw her as his best friend.

Creative Outlets

During high school, Depp tried to fit in, but without much success. His classmates called him nicknames, such as "Johnny Dip" and "Dippity-Do."

▲ *Johnny Depp is pictured in 1988 with Nicolas Cage.*

Depp's rebellious style emerged early. He got into trouble for breaking rules or behaving in dangerous ways. Part of this rebellion came from his unstable home life. Depp wasn't thinking about the consequences his actions might have.

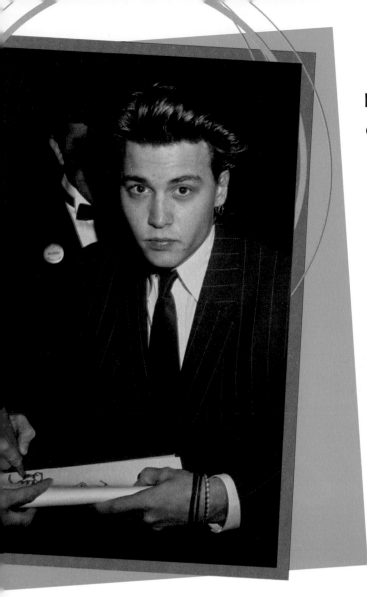

▲ Johnny Depp attends a benefit in Los Angeles, California, in 1988.

MAKING MUSIC

Depp's dream of becoming a career musician continued to grow. His love of music helped him to get through his parents' breakup and the other challenges of growing up. Depp dropped out of high school to follow his musical dream. Later, he regretted not finishing his education.

In the early 1980s, Depp started playing music with friends. They created a group called the Flame. He would make $25 each night he performed. Then Depp joined a band called The Kids. He played a 1956 Fender Telecaster guitar.

Playing in a band gave him a sense of safety he had not experienced at home. The band played all over Florida. They opened for well-known acts such as the Pretenders and R.E.M.

FIRST LOVE

In 1983, when Depp was 20, he married his first love. Lori Anne Allison was a makeup artist who was five years older than Depp. The band then decided to seek better opportunities. They moved to Los Angeles and changed their name from The Kids to Six Gun Method.

But life in Los Angeles wasn't easy. The band competed against all the other small bands in California. To earn money, Depp worked in construction and as a mechanic. He also became a telemarketer. He sold clocks to people over the phone.

Depp hated the work. But he did it because he needed the money. He also took a job selling ballpoint pens to people over the phone. He was only making $100 per week.

BREAKING INTO ACTING

Depp was only married to Lori Anne Allison for two years, but she had a huge effect on his life. She encouraged him to act. Allison introduced Depp to a young actor named Nicolas Cage. Cage was impressed with Depp, despite the fact that Depp had never done any acting. Cage decided to put Depp into contact with his agent.

Soon, Depp got a small part in Wes Craven's *A Nightmare on Elm Street* (1984). Craven said he was struck by Depp's "quiet charisma." It didn't hurt that Craven's teenaged daughter thought Depp was good looking. Struck by his daughter's reaction, Craven gave Depp the part.

Depp still wanted to be a musician. But he realized that he could make money as an actor. He planned to go back to making music as soon as possible. Unfortunately, his band broke up while he was working on the film.

NEW DIRECTION

After a few years, Depp was headed down an unexpected career path—acting. He started to take acting classes at the Loft Studio in Beverly Hills, California, and studied with a coach. He read books about acting to improve his skills.

His next important role was in a 1986 movie called *Platoon*. Made by Oliver Stone, *Platoon* was an extremely realistic war movie. Stone wanted the actors to get into the mindset of soldiers, so they went through almost two weeks of intense physical training. They were instructed by an army captain who treated them like new recruits. They went on sixty-mile hikes, slept outside, and ate cold food. The reality of being

▼ *Johnny Depp, pictured in 1990, has been a rebel since his youth.*

a soldier in wartime Vietnam hit the actors hard. All of them became ill at some point.

Depp had a small part as a translator in the film. He studied the Vietnamese language for the role. In the end, much of Depp's part was cut. But *Platoon* showed him the effect films could have on people's lives.

In 1986, Depp returned to making music for a while. It was something he had never wanted to give up. He joined a band called the Rock City Angels. However, the new world of acting reopened its doors to him.

21 JUMP STREET

People had noticed his handsome appearance and natural acting ability. In 1987, the producers of a new television show, *21 Jump Street,* approached him. Depp did not really want to be on television. But he did like the idea of acting as an undercover cop who helps teens in trouble. He was offered $45,000 per episode. That was money he couldn't make playing music. He was also reunited with a good friend from his childhood. Sal Jenco became part of the cast.

HATS OFF

Johnny Depp often wears unusual, sometimes old-fashioned, hats. When he was asked about his hat choices, he joked, "Maybe I just read too much Dr. Seuss as a kid."

But he has also been known to give his hats away. While Depp was filming in Oshkosh, Wisconsin, in April 2008, a twelve-year-old boy approached him and asked for the hat he happened to be wearing.

Depp replied that after he was finished wearing the hat, he would send it to the boy. Sure enough, later that spring, the boy's family received a package. It contained a worn tan fedora, along with a variety of souvenir items from Depp's movie *Charlie and the Chocolate Factory*.

▶ Johnny Depp sports one of his trademark hats at a premiere in 2008.

The show was filmed in Vancouver, British Columbia. As the success of *21 Jump Street* skyrocketed in 1987, Depp's personal popularity soared. It became difficult for him to have a private life. He received thousands of fan letters every week. Photos of him appeared in one teen magazine after another.

It was difficult to be known as a teen idol for several reasons. Depp didn't feel that he was much of a role model for teenagers. He had gone through some difficult times of his own. Also, he had trouble with the idea of being a star. He valued his privacy intensely. While *21 Jump Street* made him famous, Depp didn't want to spend his entire career acting on a television series.

In 1990, the show's producer released Depp from his five-year contract. Depp went on to make the movie *Cry-Baby*. The movie allowed him to make fun of his teen-idol image. He also earned $1 million for acting in the film.

Teen Idol to Serious Actor

Depp's major movie break came in the offbeat film *Edward Scissorhands* in 1990. Tim Burton directed it. Depp felt he could relate to the title character. Edward Scissorhands is

▲ *Johnny Depp appears in* Edward Scissorhands *in 1990.*

lonely and very much an outsider in the suburbs. He meets a middle-aged saleswoman, who takes him under her wing. She brings him home to live with her family. In the end, however, Edward ends up alone.

As Edward, Depp expresses a combination of innocence and sadness.

▲ *Johnny Depp is pictured at the International Film Festival in 1992.*

He communicates with limited speech. According to Depp, he used Charlie Chaplin as a model. Chaplin acted in silent movies in the early 1900s. Chaplin's characters are widely recognized. Depp appreciated Chaplin's ability to show feelings just by using his body, eyes, and facial expressions.

CREDITS

Johnny Depp has performed in more than three dozen movies and has starred in a popular television series. Here are some of the highlights of his career:

Film debut: *A Nightmare on Elm Street* (1984)
Television stardom: *21 Jump Street* (1987)
Big-screen breakthrough: *Edward Scissorhands* (1990)
Playing the outsider: *Benny & Joon* (1993), *What's Eating Gilbert Grape* (1993), *Ed Wood* (1994), *Chocolat* (2000)
Launch of a franchise: *Pirates of the Caribbean: Curse of the Black Pearl* (2003)
Family fare: *Finding Neverland* (2004), *Charlie and the Chocolate Factory* (2005), *Corpse Bride* (2005)

Believe it or not, Depp also based his character on a dog. The unconditional love given by dogs was a trait Depp thought Edward should have. Depp also had to learn to use his scissor-like hands effectively. He practiced often, while wearing his uncomfortable leather costume. All his hard work paid off. Depp received his first Golden Globe nomination for the performance.

Depp took on a variety of roles that proved his ability to find the deeper side of characters. Depp fought the typical glamorous image that his handsome looks would suggest. He took on roles that went against that stereotype.

PLAYING THE OUTSIDER

For the next two years, Depp had no problem finding interesting work. In 1993, Depp went to great lengths to get into character for *Benny & Joon*. In the movie, Benny and Joon are brother and sister. Depp plays Sam, an uneducated man who stays with them. He becomes close to Joon, who is a talented but troubled artist.

▲ *Johnny Depp appears as Sam in* Benny & Joon.

In this film, Depp had to communicate strong feelings with little dialogue. The character interacts with others using mostly facial expressions and physical tricks. Depp studied with a mime and based some of his acrobatics on those once performed by Charlie Chaplin. His work earned him a second Golden Globe nomination.

What's Eating Gilbert Grape opened in 1993. Depp starred alongside Leonardo DiCaprio. DiCaprio plays a teenager with disabilities who depends heavily on his older brother, Gilbert, and on his two sisters. Depp played Gilbert.

Depp's character struggles between his need for freedom and his sense of responsibility to his family. Like several of his other movies, *What's Eating Gilbert Grape* deals with the

▶ *Johnny Depp and Leonardo DiCaprio attend a premiere in 1993.*

THE ROLES HE DIDN'T TAKE

Even when he was a young actor, Johnny Depp turned down high-paying roles if he didn't feel he was right for the part. For instance, he rejected the lead role in *Speed*, which went to Keanu Reeves. He also turned down parts in *Legends of the Fall* and *Interview with the Vampire*, both of which went to Brad Pitt. He even turned down the lead in *Titanic*. The movie, starring Leonardo DiCaprio, became a huge hit.

theme of what it's like to be an outsider.

ED WOOD

Around the same time, Tim Burton approached Depp about a new film project, based on a true story. In *Ed Wood* (1994), Depp played an unsuccessful director who just loved filmmaking. Wood didn't have much money—or talent.

He believed that he would someday become a directing legend. Depp played Wood with sympathy. He showed Ed Wood as a man who really cared about what he was doing. Depp's acting helped the audience relate to a man who was mostly a failure. Depp received another Golden Globe nomination for his performance.

4

Life in the Spotlight

Depp has acknowledged that the late 1980s and early 1990s were a difficult time for him. He struggled with being in the spotlight. He also had problems with substance abuse.

▲ *Johnny Depp smiles after receiving an Honorary César Award in 1999 for his body of work.*

▲ *Johnny Depp waves to the crowd at a screening of* The Brave *in 1997.*

While it affected his personal life, his career was continuing successfully. Depp's celebrity status was growing.

Between 1993 and 1995, Depp returned more actively to playing music. He formed a band that included his friend Sal Jenco. The band, called P, played at the Austin Music Awards in 1993. That year, Depp also opened a music club called The Viper Room in West Hollywood, California. It was a place where Depp and his band could play and enjoy music. Other musicians, such as Johnny Cash, Bruce Springsteen, and Sheryl Crow, would drop by to jam.

P released an album in 1995, and the musicians still play together on occasion. In 1997, Depp recorded with the band Oasis. A member of Oasis called Depp "one of the best guitarists" ever. In 2003, Depp combined his love for music with his acting career. In *Once Upon a Time in Mexico*, he acted, and wrote and performed a song for the movie.

GIVING BACK

Another long-standing interest of Depp's has been his commitment to charitable causes. From an early stage in his career, he has been involved with the Make-A-Wish Foundation. He also assists the Starlight Foundation. Depp has appeared in several public service announcements to speak out against drug use.

In 1995, he appeared in a PBS special titled *The United States of Poetry*. He read the work of Jack Kerouac, one of his favorite authors. On the set, he met and befriended Kerouac's longtime friend, poet Allen Ginsberg.

▶ *Johnny Depp attends a film festival in 1997.*

29

FOR THE CHILDREN

Like many celebrities, Johnny Depp feels it is important to give back. He is especially drawn to charities that benefit children.

Make-A-Wish Foundation
An organization that grants wishes to children with life-threatening medical conditions.

Starlight Children's Foundation
A foundation that works to improve the quality of life for children with severe medical conditions by providing entertainment and activities to help them cope.

War Child
A network of organizations that provide emergency aid and long-term programs to improve the living conditions of children affected by war.

FAMILY AND FRIENDS

Depp's relationship with his mother has remained strong over the years. Depp says he admires her strength, her intelligence, and her sense of humor.

Depp has also stayed close with his other family members. His sister Christi organizes his schedule. His brother Danny co-wrote *The Brave* with him. Depp directed the film in 1997. His other sister, Debbie, lives a quieter life. Depp has reconnected with his father as well.

Depp's friends have included famous

actors Martin Landau and the late Marlon Brando. Depp worked with Brando in *Don Juan DeMarco* and later in *The Brave*.

ACTING CHOICES

Depp has often made choices about roles based on whether they felt right to him. Additionally, Depp has based his decisions on which directors he likes. He has a long history of working with director Tim Burton, for example. Depp feels he and Burton share a similar outlook on life.

▶ *Johnny Depp walks on his star on the Hollywood Walk of Fame in 1999.*

31

BUSINESS VENTURES

Johnny Depp created a production company called Infinitum Nihil in 2004. Translated from Latin, the name means "absolutely nothing." The formation of the company allows him to finance and produce movies of his choosing. His sister Christi helps run the organization. Depp also is a part owner of restaurants in Paris and New York.

Depp worked again with Burton on *Sleepy Hollow*. The movie is based on the classic tale by Washington Irving. Depp plays a detective named Ichabod Crane. The detective explores mysterious horrors in a small town in upstate New York. The film opened in 1999 and did well in theaters.

In *Chocolat* (2000), directed by Lasse Hallström, Depp's onscreen time was minimal—about 17 minutes—but he made the most of it. Again, Depp has the role of an outsider. He plays a gypsy named Roux. Roux forms a relationship with other outsiders. These include a woman who makes chocolates and her daughter, who has an imaginary kangaroo for a pet.

Chocolat is also notable because Depp plays his guitar in the movie. It is one of the few times that he has been able to combine onscreen his interests in music and acting. Depp's guitar playing also appears on the movie's soundtrack.

LOOKING FOR INSPIRATION

Depp often bases a character on something or someone familiar to him. For biographical or historical films, he spends time with the subjects of the movies or reads everything he can about the topic. Depp also uses music to inspire his acting. As he explains, "Listening to music is the quickest way to get to an emotional place I need to be in to act."

The actor doesn't hesitate to take on difficult roles. He notes that he has "a drive in me that won't allow me to do certain things that are easy."

Younger actors often look to people such as Johnny Depp for inspiration. He reminds young actors to stay in control of the work they do. He thinks they should never compromise.

Home at Last

Johnny Depp has spent much of his life longing for a sense of home. It appears he finally has found that feeling of stability. Depp has been in a relationship with French singer and

▲ *Johnny Depp and his longtime partner Vanessa Paradis arrive at the 2008 Academy Awards.*

actress Vanessa Paradis since 1998. The couple has two children, Lily-Rose Melody Depp and John "Jack" Christopher Depp III. Lily-Rose was born in 1999, and Jack was born in 2002. Paradis is well known in France for her musical hit, "Joe le taxi," which she recorded in 1987. She has also acted in several films.

Depp says that his family has provided the stability he has always sought. He admits now that years of frustration had led him to destructive actions, including substance abuse. He says that the birth of his daughter finally grounded him and taught him what was truly meaningful.

The family lives in rural France, where Depp enjoys the peaceful surroundings. Privacy laws in France protect him and his family from the media. He has said that the French seem less obsessed with movie stars than Americans.

For Depp, living in the French countryside has been nearly perfect. He has said he can live "a simple life. [I] can go to the market, walk about, buy fruits and vegetables." In addition to the country house, Depp and his family have homes in Paris, in California, and on a private island he purchased.

PLAYING A PIRATE

Having children inspired him to make the highly successful *Pirates of the Caribbean* movies. He wanted to make films his children could enjoy.

The first Pirates movie was *Pirates of the Caribbean: Curse of the Black Pearl* in 2003. In the film, Depp plays Captain Jack Sparrow, a pirate seeking to regain his lost ship. Sparrow breaks the law and steals money for his own good. On the other hand, he has a code of honor and is loyal to his friends and shipmates.

The success of the first *Pirates* movie was enormous. The film made more than $600 million. Two sequels quickly followed the first *Pirates* movie: *Pirates of the Caribbean: Dead Man's Chest* in 2006 and *Pirates of the Caribbean: At World's End* in 2007.

FAMILY-FRIENDLY FILMS

Depp finds working on children's films refreshing. Even director Tim Burton has said that fatherhood has made Depp a better, more focused actor. That is part of the reason Burton chose to cast Depp as Willy Wonka in the 2005 version of

▲ *Johnny Depp as Captain Jack Sparrow in* Pirates of the Caribbean: Dead Man's Chest.

Charlie and the Chocolate Factory. Burton also said he chose Depp because he knew Depp would bring something unexpected to the work.

WHAT THE CRITICS HAVE SAID

Johnny Depp did more than win over audiences with his portrayal of Jack Sparrow in the *Pirates of the Caribbean* movies. He also impressed many movie critics with his unusual take on the pirate.

Roger Ebert, *Chicago Sun-Times*: "His performance is original in its every atom. There has never been a pirate, or for that matter a human being, like this in any other movie."

Paul Clinton, CNN: "Much of the success of this venture can be attributed to the outstanding cast—especially Johnny Depp. . . . The film's considerable wit and humor is largely conveyed through his exquisitely eccentric character."

James Berardinelli, *Reelviews*: "*Pirates of the Caribbean* belongs to Johnny Depp. . . . With several gold teeth in his mouth and beads in his hair, Depp plays the part with an engaging goofiness that sets the movie's tone."

The movie came out in 2005, but it was a remake of a much older movie. Gene Wilder, who had stamped the role with his unique personality, had originally created the character of Willy Wonka in 1971. Depp has said he based his version of Willy Wonka on television game show hosts. And he admits that there was a bit of a "bratty child" blended in there as well.

Of course, not every movie Depp stars in is suitable for the entire family. In 2007, Depp was cast in *Sweeney Todd: The Demon Barber of Fleet Street*.

The movie is both a musical and a horror movie. Although Depp has never been very interested in acting in a musical, *Sweeney Todd* was unusual. As a horror movie, it appealed to Depp's darker side. Depp has been widely praised for his performance.

SURPRISED BY SUCCESS

Depp has come a long way since his rebellious youth. His early years did not provide a roadmap for what was to come later in life. For many years, he says, "I was convinced I had absolutely no talent at all. . . . And that thought took away all my ambition."

Of course, plenty of people would disagree that Depp has "no talent." He has been honored several times for his work. In 1999, Depp received an Honorary César Award for his body of work. The César Award is the film award of France, similar to the Academy Awards in the United States.

Depp was nominated in 2004 for an Academy Award for Best Actor for the first *Pirates* movie. It was his first Oscar nomination. He did not win, but he did win a Screen Actors Guild Award for the role.

Depp was asked in September 2005 to make handprints in the cement at Mann's Chinese Theater in Hollywood. This is a long-standing Hollywood tradition. The handprints (and sometimes footprints) of many of the film industry's best actors and actresses appear there.

Also in 2005, Depp was nominated for a second Academy Award for *Finding Neverland*. He received his third Academy Award nomination for *Sweeney Todd* in 2008.

HELPING OUT

In addition to his acting, Depp's participation in charitable events has grown. He has been honored by the Los Angeles Children's Hospital. The hospital awarded him the Courage to Care Award in 2006 for his commitment to children and children's causes. Depp also works with War Child, a group that helps children affected by war.

In 2008, Depp got back together with his band from many years ago—The Kids—to play a benefit concert. The concert raised money for the Dan Marino Foundation. The foundation supports programs for children with special needs, such as autism. Depp has said he feels that children

HONORS

Johnny Depp loves to take on challenging roles, and many people have praised his ability to play different characters. His work has earned him recognition a number of times. Here is a sampling of Depp's honors:

- Won a Golden Globe for Best Performance by an Actor in a Motion Picture—Musical or Comedy: *Sweeney Todd: The Demon Barber of Fleet Street* (2008)
- Won a Kids' Choice Award for Favorite Male Movie Star: *Pirates of the Caribbean: At World's End* (2008)
- Won a Screen Actors Guild Award for Outstanding Performance by a Male Actor in a Leading Role: *Pirates of the Caribbean: Curse of the Black Pearl* (2004)
- Nominated for three Academy Awards for Best Performance by an Actor in a Leading Role: *Sweeney Todd: The Demon Barber of Fleet Street* (2008), *Finding Neverland* (2005), and *Pirates of the Caribbean: Curse of the Black Pearl* (2004)
- Nominated for six Golden Globes for Best Performance by an Actor in a Motion Picture—Musical or Comedy: *Pirates of the Caribbean: Dead Man's Chest* (2007), *Charlie and the Chocolate Factory* (2006), *Pirates of the Caribbean: Curse of the Black Pearl* (2004), *Ed Wood* (1995), *Benny & Joon* (1994), and *Edward Scissorhands* (1991)
- Nominated for a Golden Globe for Best Performance by an Actor in a Motion Picture—Drama: *Finding Neverland* (2005)

facing disease are the "most courageous people I've ever met."

FINDING MEANING

As he has gotten older, Depp appears to have become more comfortable in his own skin. He loves his family, and his acting career continues to be successful. He has found meaning in making movies that appeal to him, and in supporting causes that are important to him.

Depp's fame and fortune seem to grow stronger every year. Still, he makes decisions in a similar way to when he had little money and hardly anyone knew his name. Depp looks for movies that have interesting characters who inspire his creativity.

Often, Depp has taken on characters who have struggled or have experienced being the outsider. The roles he plays seem to echo his own struggles and ambitions. His commitment to respecting differences is reflected in the work he has chosen to do and in the life he has chosen to live.

Johnny Depp attends the 2006 Golden Globe Awards. He was ▶
nominated for his role in Charlie and the Chocolate Factory.

Timeline

1963 John Christopher Depp II is born in Owensboro, Kentucky

1975 Receives his first guitar from his mother

1984 Lands a minor role in *A Nightmare on Elm Street*

1987 Gets a major acting break on *21 Jump Street*

1990 Stars in his first major motion picture, *Edward Scissorhands*

1993 Appears in *Benny & Joon* and *What's Eating Gilbert Grape*

1995 Releases an album as part of the rock group P

1998 Begins dating singer-actress Vanessa Paradis

1999 Given a star on the Hollywood Walk of Fame

2003 Stars in *Pirates of the Caribbean: Curse of the Black Pearl*

2005 Stars in the remake of *Charlie and the Chocolate Factory*

2008 Earns his third Academy Award nomination for *Sweeney Todd*

Further Info

Books

Graziano, Jim. *Johnny Depp*. Broomall, PA: Mason Crest Publishers, 2008.

Singer, Michael. *Bring Me That Horizon: The Making of Pirates of the Caribbean*. New York: Disney Editions, 2007.

Thomas, William David. *Johnny Depp*. Milwaukee, WI: Gareth Stevens Publishing, 2007.

CDs and DVDs

A&E Biography: Johnny Depp. Los Angeles: Twentieth Century Fox Film Corporation, 2004.

Charlie and the Chocolate Factory. Warner Bros., 2005.

Internet Addresses

The Internet Movie Database: Johnny Depp
http://www.imdb.com/name/nm0000136/

Pirates of the Caribbean: The Official Web Site
http://disney.go.com/disneypictures/pirates/